Property of the
UNO Charter School Network
Carlos Fuentes Charter School

Red Means Good Fortune

A STORY OF SAN FRANCISCO'S CHINATOWN

BY BARBARA DIAMOND GOLDIN

ILLUSTRATED BY WENHAI MA

SCHOLASTIC INC.
New York   Toronto   London   Auckland   Sydney
Mexico City   New Delhi   Hong Kong   Buenos Aires

*Special thanks to Jonathan Lipman of Mount Holyoke College and
Cecilia Yung for reading and commenting on this text.*

No part of this publication may be reproduced in whole or in part, or stored
in a retrieval system, or transmitted in any form or by any means, electronic, mechanical, photocopying,
recording, or otherwise, without written permission of the publisher. For information regarding permission,
write to Penguin Putnam Inc., 345 Hudson Street, New York, NY 10014.

Text copyright © 1994 by Barbara Diamond Goldin.
Illustrations copyright © 1994 by Wenhai Ma.
Cover illustration copyright © 1994 by Ronald Himler.
All rights reserved. Published by Scholastic Inc., 557 Broadway, New York, NY 10012,
by arrangement with Penguin Putnam Inc.
Printed in the U.S.A.

ISBN 0-439-58285-7

SCHOLASTIC and associated logos and designs are trademarks and/or
registered trademarks of Scholastic Inc.

ONCE UPON AMERICA is a registered trademark of Viking Penguin,
a division of Penguin Putnam Inc.

2 3 4 5 6 7 8 9 10   40   12 11 10 09 08 07 06 05 04

To Nancy Carlstrom
and our Seattle Writing Group
for all the help and love—
Nancy L., and Nancy I., Margaret, Pat, Cathy,
Chris, Jody, Eileen, Linda, Judy.

Contents

Meeting Lew Wai Hing

Chin Jin Mun walked carefully down the busy street. He didn't want to drop the bundles of clean laundry. Yesterday a galloping horse had startled him and down he went. Today he would pay attention.

As his father always told him at the beginning of each day, "You can't walk carrying a big load of laundry with your head full of dreams."

But he liked thinking of the mountains Older Brother described in his letters. "When you look up in this wild land called Nevada," Older Brother wrote,

"you can see a chain of mountains that stretches forever into the sky. The light and colors of the mountains are always changing, now purple, now blue and pink."

If only his father had allowed him, too, to leave San Francisco and work on the railroad. Then he could see those mountains that reached the clouds. He could see the steep cliffs and the rivers, the bobcats and the mountain goats.

Instead, he was stuck here doing his chores. He was supposed to think only of the long pole that went across his back. He had to pay attention to the baskets that dangled from each end of the pole. Or else, what use would he be to his father—he, Jin Mun, a boy of twelve years by the white devils' counting?

At least this was his last delivery for the day. Soon he could go home to the laundry and the warm dinner cooked by his father.

Suddenly, he thought of his mother bending over him, giving him his bowl of rice in their little house in the village back home in China. A painful longing came over him.

It had been three years since he had seen his mother. He and Older Brother had traveled then in the big boat to come to this, the land of the Golden Mountain.

Father had been here even longer. He worked hard to start his own laundry. When he saved enough money, he brought his two sons over to help him. Jin Mun's mother and sisters stayed behind.

2

It was mostly the men who came here to the land of the Golden Mountain. These men all had a plan. If they worked hard, they could save enough money to return to China as rich men.

His father said, "That way, when we are back home at last, we won't worry if floods ruin the rice crop or bandits burn our fields. We will have this." Then Father would point to a floorboard in the laundry. This was to remind Jin Mun of the wooden box hidden under there where his father kept their savings.

Father would continue, "This is why we mustn't cut off our queues." He would touch the long, sleek, black pigtail that dangled all the way down his back. "We must keep them so we can return to our home. That is the Emperor's law."

It was because of Father's plan that Older Brother had gone off to join Crocker's railroad crew. They chipped away at the mountains to build the Central Pacific Railroad.

And it was because of this plan that Father cooked with only a little meat and fish. And why he stopped going to the fan-tan table, where men lost their savings in gambling games.

Jin Mun stopped to make his next delivery. It was to the new restaurant on the corner of Dupont and Sacramento streets.

He walked past the restaurant to the basement steps next door. Lifting the baskets off his pole, he carried them and the pole down the steps. He knocked on the wooden door.

Inside, he could hear an old woman's voice calling, "See who's there, you lazy girl. Hurry!"

He heard footsteps. The door opened a little and he saw a small, pretty face peering at him.

"Is this where Wong Lo You lives? I've brought his clean laundry," Jin Mun said.

The girl nodded silently. She lifted the laundry from the baskets. Jin Mun guessed she was a little younger than he was. Perhaps she was ten or eleven years old by the white devils' counting.

"You may come in while I get the dirty things," she said quietly. But as she began to run with the bundles, she lost her balance and fell.

"Let me help you," Jin Mun said. He reached for one of the bundles.

"No," the girl said in a whisper. "My mistress will be angry." She pointed to a room off the hallway.

"She won't know," Jin Mun whispered.

Jin Mun left his pole and baskets by the door. Then he carried one bundle and the girl the other. They went down the dark hallway to the kitchen.

"Put it here," she said, "by the stove."

As Jin Mun put the bundle down, he noticed the picture of the Kitchen God above the stove. The old man in his blue and red robes smiled down at him. It

was the same picture Jin Mun and his father had in their laundry.

"It's like ours," he said to the girl.

She smiled shyly. Her face took on a thoughtful look. "When I burn incense and candles before his shrine, I pray that he will hear my prayers. I pray he will report them in heaven," she said.

Jin Mun wondered what it was this pretty, serious girl prayed for. A new *sohm,* a blouse, perhaps? Hers was so thin and old. Or some sweet cakes and ginger candies? A bright lantern for these dark basement rooms?

The girl pointed to the bundle of dirty laundry.

"For you to take," she said. "And thanks for helping me. Usually I do everything all by myself."

"Your mistress? Is she very old then?" Jin Mun asked.

"Yes. And she has the little feet."

Jin Mun nodded. He had seen women with bound feet here in San Francisco and at home in China, too. These women could barely walk, let alone do housework. When he was small, he had asked his mother about the tiny feet of some of the women. He saw them carried in sedan chairs down the road near his village.

"Lily feet," his mother called them. "It's a very old tradition. Small feet are considered beautiful." She lifted up her foot, a farmer's wife's foot. "My big feet are ugly. If a mother hopes to marry her daughter to a wealthy man, she binds the toes under and bends them with cloths when the girl is very young. Lovely lily feet mean a rich mother-in-law."

Jin Mun wiggled his toes and shuddered. How painful it had to be!

Suddenly he heard giggling. It was coming from the servant girl.

"What's so funny?"

"You were staring at your feet. Wiggling them," she said.

Jin Mun blushed.

"Oh no. Don't feel bad," the girl said quickly. "It's a good thing. To be funny. To laugh. I like it. But my mistress"—the girl shook her head from side to side—"she doesn't like it."

"Your mistress sounds very bad-tempered," Jin Mun said.

"She is," agreed the girl.

"Well, I guess I'd better go. My father is waiting for me," Jin Mun said.

They walked quietly back down the long hallway. At the door, Jin Mun took his pole and put the new bundle in one of the baskets.

"I'll help you when I come again," he said. "My name is Chin Jin Mun."

"My name is Lew Wai Hing," whispered the girl. "It's nice to have someone to talk to."

"Oh. You don't have any friends here yet?"

"Not one," Wai Hing answered.

"Couldn't you meet another girl when you go visiting or on Lantern Day or . . ."

Wai Hing interrupted him. "You don't understand," she said. "I don't go anywhere. I'm the mistress's slave, her *mui tsai*. She doesn't let me step outside her door."

"Never?" Jin Mun asked.

"Never."

Chin Jin Mun's World

All the way down the street, Wai Hing's words troubled him. Imagine! Never to be allowed outside!

Looking about him, Jin Mun noticed things he usually paid no attention to. He saw the shop windows. Each one opened onto a different world. One was filled with dried fish and salted cabbage, hanging ducks and ginger root. Another displayed carefully carved wooden figures, and vases and scrolls decorated with scenes of mountains, streams, and villages.

He felt a little guilty. Just before he had been so

sorry for himself because he couldn't join Older Brother in the mountains. He had to do these deliveries and carry this heavy pole. And here was Wai Hing shut up in those dark rooms. She was like a prisoner.

Jin Mun passed one of his favorite spots, the corner where the lantern maker sat. His gold and red strips of paper and bamboo would quickly, almost magically, become shapely lanterns.

A toy peddler walked by. He was pulling tiny carts filled with dolls. As two children turned their heads to see, the bright golden devil chasers sewn into their caps jingled.

Fly away, devils of the air! Chase you! Chase you! Hear the noise? Away! Away! the jingling of their caps seemed to say.

This world of the toy peddler, the lantern maker, and the shop windows is closed to Lew Wai Hing, thought Jin Mun. That's much worse than not being able to see the mountains or having to carry this awful pole.

I'll tell Father about Lew Wai Hing. Maybe we can help her.

He pushed open the door to the laundry. The steamy air inside greeted him. His father was standing in front of a big table, holding a hot iron. Lines of drying shirts and sheets crisscrossed the room. In a corner stood a big wooden tub filled with water.

"All done?" his father asked. "I've been waiting for you." He was small and thin and seemed always to be bending over, even when he was away from the ironing. "Your rice is cooked so you can eat and go to evening school."

"I'm done, Father." Jin Mun sat down on a stool near the table.

"Father," Jin Mun said between mouthfuls. "That customer, Wong Lo You, has a slave girl. Her name is Lew Wai Hing."

His father kept ironing.

"The poor girl is never allowed to go out."

"There are many slave girls," his father said. He never once stopped the back-and-forth motion of the iron. "You know that."

"Yes, I know. But I never talked to one before. . . ."

"No. They are often kept hidden away, so no one will see them and steal them."

Jin Mun held some rice in the chopsticks in front of his mouth. He could not eat.

"Little Brother, eat your food," his father said.

"It is a mean thing to keep her locked up. I would hate it."

"You do not have to worry. You're a boy. Try to understand the way it is back home. There, if a family is poor and their rice crop fails once again, they starve.

"The father knows he can get much money for his girl child. He is sometimes tempted.

"He thinks—she will go live with another family anyway, with her husband's family, as soon as she is married. And he will not see her very often.

"He thinks—she will offer food and incense to her new family's ancestors, not ours.

"He thinks—oh, he thinks many things when he and his family are starving. Understand, Little Brother?"

Jin Mun put the rice down. "No, I don't understand, Father."

"You are in this country only a short time and already you do not understand the way we do things back home. Well, maybe it's a good thing you do not understand such starving. But I have seen it in my own village.

"Why do you think I am here, far away from our family? It is so I can work hard and send money home each month. Then this will not happen to *your* sisters."

"But what can we do about Lew Wai Hing?" Jin Mun persisted.

"There is nothing we can do. In this country, it costs $600, $800, $1000 to buy a slave girl or to free one." He looked at his son. "Now go to school and come back quickly. Then you can read Older Brother's new letter to me."

Jin Mun jumped off the stool. "Oh, please, Father. Let me see the letter now," he begged.

"No. You must not miss school. It is important to learn English, as well as having lessons from Sam Lock in writing the Chinese characters. Knowing both will help you in this country and then when we return home. Go. And forget about that slave girl."

Older Brother's Letter

Jin Mun was cold walking back from the missionary school. He wrapped his blue padded cotton jacket tightly around him.

He had struggled for over an hour with the English. Mr. Christiansen, the teacher, had explained a new word, a long one—*opportunity*. He said that this new land was filled with opportunity. He said a person could be anything he wanted to be in this country if he worked hard enough.

"It's not like in China," Mr. Christiansen said.

"There if you are born a farmer, you are always a farmer. Here you can change. You can choose."

The new word excited Jin Mun. It was the same kind of feeling he had when he read Older Brother's letters about the mountains.

Older Brother! He had almost forgotten. Jin Mun started running. He ran toward the laundry and Older Brother's letter.

"Respected Father and Little Brother," the letter began. "I hope you are well and staying warm.

"It is cold here. Colder than it ever is in San Francisco or at home. We are covered with snow and must work in tunnels under the snow.

"You may wonder why our boss, Crocker, keeps us working. It is because of the big race I have told you about, the race between us and the Union Pacific Railroad. That is the other train line coming from the East to meet us.

"The harder we work, and the more track we lay, the more money this railroad, the Central Pacific Railroad, makes. Each mile of track is worth thousands of dollars.

"The government wants a railroad to connect the West of this huge country with the East. And so it pays much to the owners to build it.

"Crocker hired Mr. Brown, a bridge builder. Brown showed Crocker how to build wooden tunnels. Crocker ordered 40 miles of these tunnels built. It is much safer to haul and dig and lay track under these wood tunnels than under ones made only of snow.

"Can you imagine, Little Brother, that we eat and sleep and work in these dark tunnels day after day? Maybe you will not be so jealous of me now, out here in the mountains."

Jin Mun stopped reading. He thought about what his brother said. No. I still wish I could see those tunnels and all that snow. But . . .

"Why do you stop, Little Brother?" asked his father.

"I wonder. Do you think Older Brother is safe in these tunnels?"

"Probably safer than he was in those baskets."

Jin Mun shuddered. Father was right. How they had worried about Older Brother after that letter. The workers had reached a sheer cliff. Crocker told them a tunnel had to be made through the rock of the cliff so the train could go through to the other side. His Chinese crews had proved themselves to be clever and hardworking. Crocker hoped they would be able to figure out a way.

To Crocker's surprise, the workers began to shave long, thin strips of wood off lumber and weave them into baskets that could hold two men.

The workers then lowered these baskets over the side of the cliff with ropes. Hundreds of feet in the air, the men used chisels and hammers to chip away

at the rock. Sometimes the ropes broke and the baskets went tumbling. The men inside were killed.

Jin Mun sighed and picked up the letter again.

"Everything sleeps here in the winter," he read, "except for us, drilling and hammering, shoveling, sawing, and chipping away. We are breaking the silence of this untouched land with our noise. How we are changing it!

"Crocker says the work will be much easier on the other side of this mountain. It should be just a couple of months more until we meet the other railroad.

"But first comes the New Year. I am writing Mother a New Year's letter too. And don't worry, Father. I am saving money to help fill the box."

Jin Mun finished reading the letter.

"He sounds good," said his father.

"He does," answered Jin Mun. "Are you going to bed, Father?"

"It's time for you, too."

"I *am* tired," said Jin Mun. "The laundry baskets are heavy."

But Jin Mun could not fall asleep. Older Brother's talk of the snow tunnels made Jin Mun think of Wai Hing living in those dark basement rooms. They were like tunnels under the ground. Maybe Older Brother can understand how I feel about this poor slave girl, thought Jin Mun.

Maybe Older Brother will want to help her! I'll write him. He'll help me come up with a plan. He and his friends figured out how to lower themselves in baskets and chip away at a sheer cliff. They'll be able to figure out how to free one slave girl.

Trouble

Jin Mun wrote Older Brother a letter. It was hard to wait until his next laundry delivery to Wong Lo You. He wanted to speak to Wai Hing. He would tell her how they would be able to work out a plan to free her.

"Have you finished Wong Lo You's laundry yet?" Jin Mun asked his father.

His father looked at him, but said only, "You can take it back today. Make sure he pays you for the last time."

Jin Mun fixed his pole. He placed one basket on each end, and began walking to Mr. Wong's.

The door opened. Jin Mun was greeted by a bony-cheeked face, with a cigarette dangling out of the mouth.

It must be the master, Wong Lo You himself, Jin Mun thought. Now I'll never get a chance to talk to Wai Hing.

"What is it?" the bony-faced one said sharply. "What do you want?"

"Uncle Wong, I am Chin Jin Mun, the delivery boy." He gave the man the bundle.

Wong Lo You grunted. "Wait here. I will see what else we have for you and pay you."

"Excuse me, but for last time, too," said Jin Mun.

Soon the man came back and gave Jin Mun the dirty laundry and the coins.

Mr. Wong shut the door, but Jin Mun could not move. After a few minutes, he walked back up the stairs and past the restaurant. He just stood there, waiting and watching and thinking. The front door opened again. The master climbed up the stairs and went into his restaurant.

Maybe now I can talk to Wai Hing and no one will know, Jin Mun thought.

Softly, quietly, he turned into the alley behind the restaurant.

Bending over, he looked into a window. He could see it was the kitchen Wai Hing had shown him.

He tapped on the glass. Nothing happened. He bent down, found a few small stones, and threw them onto the window ledge. They made a *ping ping* sound.

Someone stared up at him. It was Wai Hing. She looked startled.

He made a motion with his hand, a lifting-up motion.

She looked around her. Then she climbed onto a stool and raised the window as far as she could, which was barely a crack. He could move it no farther himself.

"It's probably been nailed down," he whispered.

She nodded, agreeing.

"I was afraid I wouldn't be able to speak to you," Wai Hing whispered. "You came when the master was still here. Even now, we have only a minute. The mistress won't like it if she finds out I'm talking with you."

"I have to talk to you," Jin Mun said. "I have an idea."

"For what?" Wai Hing looked puzzled.

"To help you run away," Jin Mun told her. "My brother works on the railroad. He's very clever. When he comes back, we will free you."

Wai Hing slumped down on the stool. "It will never work. Men are always sent out to find a slave who runs

away. Don't you know this? Then the master beats her. No, it won't work."

"If they find us, we'll tell the police."

"You just don't know, Jin Mun. I heard all the stories while I was waiting to be sold. The master pays the police. If he is brought before a judge, he just says, 'That girl is my niece.' And they let him take her back."

The hope went out of Jin Mun's face.

"I could be in worse places," she said.

"If only I had the money to buy you your freedom."

Wai Hing sighed. "You are a dreamer. How could a boy get so much money? No. This is my bad luck."

She sighed again. "It wasn't always this way. I have a mother and a father at home."

"They sold you?"

Wai Hing shook her head. "No. I was taken from them. One day an old lady came to our house. My mother felt sorry for her. She gave her a bowl of rice and let her sleep in our yard.

"In the night, I awoke, feeling cold air blow in on me. Then, before I could cry out, a heavy cloth smelling of medicine was pressed against my face."

Wai Hing stopped.

"Don't stop," pleaded Jin Mun.

"I must listen for the mistress," she said. They were quiet. There was no sound, so she continued.

"What I remember next is being dragged toward a

big boat. I had never seen a boat before. I was very scared. I cried for my mother.

"The old woman slapped me. 'If you cry again, I will throw you out there, in the water. The sea dragon will eat you!'

"We went onto that big boat and stayed on it for many weeks. It was an awful journey.

"Now," Wai Hing said, "my parents do not know where I am."

She sighed. "You must go now. But thank you for your plan. Next time, make me laugh."

"But they *will* let you out for the New Year Festival?" Jin Mun asked. "They must!"

Wai Hing shook her head sadly. "They never have. I am just a slave girl. They think I have no feelings. They think I am like the mistress's fan or her bed warmer or her chopsticks."

"If I asked your master?" Jin Mun persisted.

"You must not!" she said. Wai Hing jumped quickly down from the stool and vanished.

Jin Mun lifted his pole and baskets and walked toward the restaurant.

"This isn't China. It's different here," Jin Mun muttered to himself. "Wong Lo You will say yes. For a holiday."

Before he knew it, Jin Mun found himself in the kitchen of the restaurant. The master was chopping cabbage with a large cleaver.

The master looked up. "What is it? You have the laundry. Well?"

Suddenly, Jin Mun was afraid. He must have been dreaming to think he could do this. He blurted out some words.

"Your *mui tsai*," he said. "Would you let her outside for the New Year Festival? At least for Lantern Day and the dragon dance? She would not be stolen away."

The old man looked right at Jin Mun.

"And what do you care about my *mui tsai?*" He had lifted the cleaver while he spoke and was shaking it at Jin Mun.

One slip and that cleaver is going to come flying right at me, Jin Mun thought.

He backed away and his pole clunked against the stove.

"What do you know about my *mui tsai?* You speak to her. Don't you? Don't you?"

"I . . . I . . . just thought it would be nice if . . . just one time . . ."

"You stay away from her," said Wong Lo You. "Don't talk to her. Ever."

Jin Mun backed away, all the way, out onto the street.

Now I've gotten Wai Hing into trouble, he thought. Her master will never let her out.

Jin Mun was so upset that he didn't think of where

he was going. He just kept walking. He didn't care what his pole hit or knocked or bumped against.

Suddenly, he felt a sharp pain in his shoulder and another on his cheek. Something whizzed by his ear.

He heard the sound of the white devils' talk. He looked around and saw three boys. They were bending over, laughing, picking up more stones. They yelled, "Chink, Chink! Go away! Go away or we'll cut off your tail!"

Jin Mun ran, without his pole, without the laundry. He ran until he found Sacramento Street and Dupont Street, then the laundry. It wasn't really very far. He was safe.

But he was in big trouble. He would have to tell his father that he had gone where he wasn't supposed to, away from the streets where his people lived. And worse, he had left the pole and the laundry behind.

And now he knew Wai Hing was right. They could never rescue her and get away. He couldn't even get a few blocks away by himself.

Father will be so angry, Jin Mun groaned. He told me to forget about Wai Hing. Now he will never agree to help free her. Never.

Just a Boy

Jin Mun stood outside the laundry door, afraid to go in. The cut on his cheek burned. And he was worried about the baskets he had left behind.

"Ai! What happened to you!" his father cried out when he saw Jin Mun.

"I got lost," Jin Mun explained. "Three white devils were after me. I dropped everything and ran."

His father took a deep breath. "Don't you listen when I tell you not to wander off? Even three blocks away makes a difference. Sit down," his father ordered.

After he filled a bowl with hot water, his father found a clean cloth and wiped all of Jin Mun's sores.

"What were you dreaming about this time? The mountains? The snow? Always dreaming . . ."

Jin Mun felt terrible, but he couldn't lie to his father. "No, not the mountains or the snow."

"Then what?"

"The girl."

His father groaned.

"I asked her master if she could come out for the lantern festival. For just one day. He was very angry. He waved his cleaver at me."

His father shook his head. "Losing laundry over a slave girl! Making a customer angry!" he muttered. "It is not your business.

"Now where are the baskets and the pole? That's your business. Was there laundry in the baskets?"

"Just one bundle, Father. And I can find the house."

"Every shirt, every sheet in that bundle is important," his father said, as he put away the irons. "They are the money we send your mother, the money we save.

"You will have to miss school tonight to show me this place. I will ask Sam Lock if we can borrow his wagon. It's safer."

Jin Mun sat next to his father in the front of the

wagon. Sam Lock's big black horse pulled them up and down the familiar streets. Clay. Commercial. Sacramento.

Then they reached the strange streets. California. Pine. Bush. His father sat straighter in the wagon. He watched not only the road in front of them, but the sides, too.

They were coming closer to the boys and the stones and the running away.

Jin Mun made himself sit up tall in the wagon. He showed his father the way. Up one street, then another. Would they ever find the laundry?

Then he saw something white behind a bush.

"Stop!" he called to his father. "This is it."

He looked all about. There was no sign of the boys. There was only a man who was crossing the street. He had a tall black hat on his head and a thick black beard.

"I'll get it," Jin Mun said. He jumped down from the wagon. He moved quickly, grabbing the bundle. The pole and the baskets were gone.

"We are lucky," his father said when Jin Mun climbed back onto the wagon. "It is the laundry that's important. Now to get home."

Cluck. Cluck. His tongue told the horse what to do. They moved forward.

There was a shout. "Hey, you! Stop!"

It was the man in the beard and black hat, shouting

and waving at them. "Thieves! What do you have there? I'll call the police."

Jin Mun's father didn't turn his head to look. "Faster!" he told the horse. "Faster!"

Neither Jin Mun nor his father spoke until they pulled up to Sam Lock's grocery.

They returned the wagon and walked together to the laundry. "I hope now you know why I told you and Older Brother to stay here on these streets, where it is safe," his father said. "Back home a son listens and obeys his father."

Jin Mun nodded, still too shaken to speak.

His father cooked the rice for dinner, and continued talking.

"I do not understand. This Lew Wai Hing is a stranger, a slave girl. There are many slave girls. Are you going to worry about every one? And what could you do? You are just a boy.

"Now I will have to make all of the deliveries to Wong Lo You's. You must not go there again. You will just make it worse for the girl."

Jin Mun knew his father was right. But maybe he could still think of a way to help Wai Hing. After all, the New Year was coming. Maybe there would be a change of luck for them both.

For the next few days, they were busy getting ready for the New Year. A week before the holiday, Jin Mun and his father took down the picture of the Kitchen

God that hung on the wall by the stove. It was black with stove smoke.

They took honey and smeared some on the Kitchen God's lips. They hoped he would remember their household with sweet thoughts on his visit to the heavens. They hoped he would report good things about them before his return on the first day of the New Year.

He watched as his father burned the Kitchen God's picture in the alley behind the laundry. He watched as the smoke and ashes rose higher and higher, sending their message upward.

Suddenly, he felt excited, very excited. Here they were sending a message with the Kitchen God. And he, Jin Mun, could be a messenger, too! He would write to Wai Hing's parents and tell them she was still alive! Maybe they would be able to help her!

There is only one trouble, he thought. How am I going to get her father's name and the name of her village if I cannot make a delivery there? If I cannot speak to her? I do not dare ask Father to find out for me.

But it is such a good idea! Jin Mun couldn't help feeling hopeful.

The Red
Lantern

A change in luck, Jin Mun kept thinking. He was helping his father clean and cook. They swept every spot in the laundry.

As was the custom, there would be no sweeping on the first few days of the New Year. They might sweep their new luck right out the door!

The New Year celebrations would begin tonight. The streets were busy as Jin Mun made the rest of his deliveries. Some people were still buying gifts. Others were settling their debts before the old year ended. Others were buying groceries and special treats like candied apricots and watermelon seeds. Tomorrow all the stores would be closed, the laundry, too.

Red, the joy color, was everywhere. There were red papers with poems written on them and red cloth draped over newly painted signs. Inside the houses and out, there was the color red.

Joy was in the air. Hope, too. The hope that this year, the year of the snake, would bring happiness, wealth, and good luck.

Jin Mun had a few coins his father had given him to buy firecrackers. After his last delivery, he looked for the peddler selling the red strings of firecrackers. You could never have enough to set off at the New Year. The more noise you made, the better. Then you would be sure to scare off the evil spirits.

Right next to the firecracker peddler was the old lantern maker.

Another lantern would be good, too, Jin Mun thought. The evil spirits did not like light either. They liked darkness.

Of all the lanterns, Jin Mun settled on a simple red one. It was nice and round with a gold design on the top and bottom. Golden fringes hung down in layers and blew around in the chilly breeze. He liked the way the light shone through the lantern with a strong red glow.

I'll buy this one for Wai Hing, he thought. It will be good luck for her.

Jin Mun paid for the lantern. The old man gave him a new one that was all folded up.

I'll slip it through her kitchen window, thought Jin Mun. And if *my* New Year luck starts early, I'll get a chance to ask Wai Hing her father's name and village, too.

Jin Mun ran all the way back to the laundry. He didn't want to have the bulky baskets and pole with him when he went to see Wai Hing.

"I'll be back soon," he called to his father. "I finished all the deliveries."

His father smiled at him. He was in a holiday mood, too.

Walking to the alley behind Mr. Wong's restaurant, Jin Mun thought about his father. About how hard his father worked.

This year, I'll try to please him more, Jin Mun decided. I'll pay attention and think ahead. But there is one thing I can't do and that is to forget my new friend.

When Jin Mun reached the alley, he looked all about to make sure there was no sign of the master or mistress. He crept to the window and threw some stones at the ledge. Suddenly, he felt sick with fear. What if Wai Hing wasn't there? What if something had happened to her? It had been days and days since he had seen her. And his father had brought no word of her. What if . . .

He was ready to run. But he didn't have to. Wai Hing got up onto the stool and lifted the window a crack. She whispered, "We are safe for a few minutes. I thought you would never come back. The master was so angry after you came last time. He said he would sell me if he ever saw me talking to you."

"I tried to stay away," said Jin Mun. "But I had to see you. I have an idea."

"Not another one!"

"Don't worry. This one won't cause you any trouble. But first, I have something for you," Jin Mun said.

He pushed the folded lantern through the crack under the window. "It will bring you light and luck."

Wai Hing accepted the lantern tenderly. "No one has given me anything like this. Not since . . ." She couldn't talk anymore.

Jin Mun felt so sorry for her.

"This idea will work," he said hopefully. "I just need your father's name and the name of your village."

"But why?"

"I'll write to him."

"That won't help." The eagerness left Wai Hing's face. "They have no money to come here to buy my freedom. They are poor farmers."

"I want to try," said Jin Mun. "Maybe they have a friend, a relative, who will help."

Wai Hing shrugged. "My father is Lew Hay Dai. He lives in the village of Gop Sak in the Toishan district of Kwangtung Province. And thank you for trying to help me, for being my friend. I must go. If they find me here, I'm afraid Wong Lo You will sell me. I'm getting older. Soon I'll be old enough to be sold for someone's wife. Or . . ." She looked worried. "I must go."

Hiding the lantern under her blouse, she got off the stool. Jin Mun watched her disappear into the darkness.

Two Letters

That night, Jin Mun wrote a letter to Wai Hing's father. With a coin he had saved, he gave the letter to Sam Lock to mail.

Jin Mun's writing was getting better now. He wrote letters home for his father and sometimes for the other men.

Every time he finished a letter, his father would smile. "A scribe in our family!" he would say. "There are some amazing things about this land of the Golden Mountain."

But where was Jin Mun's New Year luck? No letters came. No news from Older Brother or Wai Hing's parents. No new ideas came either.

One day, after they ate their rice, his father tapped Jin Mun on the shoulder.

"What is it, Little Brother?" he asked. "Is it that we haven't heard from Older Brother? Is that why you look so sad?"

Jin Mun leaned his elbows on the ironing table. "Oh, Father. I have worked so hard this New Year, but nothing has changed. There is no letter from Older Brother or from Lew Wai Hing's father."

"Lew Wai Hing's father? What father?" his own father sputtered. "What are you talking about? It's that girl again!"

Jin Mun explained everything.

"So you are still trying. And I ordered you to forget."

"I haven't," said Jin Mun. "But maybe you were right. I am just a boy and there is nothing I can do."

His father was silent for a long time. Finally he said, "She hasn't been sold, Little Brother. I saw her just the other day."

Jin Mun looked up at his father. "Really? I was worried. . . . There isn't much time. She is almost eleven by the white devils' counting. Oh, I wish there was something I could do. . . ."

"You have done something," said his father. "You

have written to her parents. Maybe something will come of that."

"But letters take so long."

His father nodded. "One learns how to be patient in this life. Look at your mother. Waiting all these years for us to come home."

Jin Mun nodded. "You miss her, don't you?"

"Very much. It is such a long time."

Jin Mun realized once again he could never ask his father for money for Wai Hing's freedom. But maybe he could ask for his help.

"Father," Jin Mun began. "Could you find out if Wong Lo You plans to sell her?"

His father looked at Jin Mun kindly. "I could," he answered.

"Maybe he would wait," said Jin Mun, getting excited now and sitting at the edge of his stool. "If we offered him something, if we said we would do his laundry for free."

"What? Never!"

"Please. I would do it. After school. And I would write letters for the others and give Wong Lo You that money, too. If only he would wait a few months."

"You'll be very busy.

"It would be better than worrying."

With a smile tugging at his mouth, his father said, "All right. I will talk to this man. But first I will make sure he isn't holding a cleaver."

Jin Mun laughed. It was good to hear his father joke again.

One cold, wet evening a few weeks later, his father said, "I have news, Little Brother. I talked to Wong Lo You. He is not in such a hurry to sell his *mui tsai* now. Not when there's free laundry and some money besides just for waiting.

"Ai! I never heard of paying someone to wait. Not back home," his father complained.

But Jin Mun kept his word. In the next few weeks, he worked all day for his father. In the evening he went to school, washed and ironed, and wrote letters.

When it was time to go to sleep, he was so tired, he had no time to dream. He had no time to think of mountains and bobcats and snow tunnels.

Then the first letter came, the one from Older Brother. Sam Lock brought it over after dinner.

"I feel sorry for this Lew Wai Hing," Older Brother wrote. "I have never thought very much about the girls who are slaves. But I don't think we can rescue her, Little Brother. There are these men—hatchet men, they are called—that the masters hire to bring back their slaves. I am not sure there is anything we can do for this girl."

Jin Mun had trouble reading the rest of the letter. Older Brother went on to say, "I have decided to stay out here, working on the railroads. Not on this line. We are all finished. I was there on the big day when they drove the last spike into the ground. This spike put the two railroads together, the one from the West and the one from the East. This new land now has a railroad that people can ride on from one great ocean to the other.

"But there are other railroads. And they all need workers. I will try to find one in the mountains, if I can.

"I will write you soon to tell you where I am working. And you must write me, too. Tell me more about this Lew Wai Hing and your hopes to free her. Maybe there is a way I can help. You certainly have big ideas, Little Brother."

Jin Mun finished reading. "I was hoping he would come back to the laundry," said his father. "But here sons make up their own minds."

"I will miss Older Brother, too," said Jin Mun. He really needed him now.

Then, in early summer the second letter came, the answer from Wai Hing's father. Sam Lock ran over with it.

"Jin Mun! The letter's come. But, ai, it is a thin one," Sam Lock called out.

Jin Mun took the letter, afraid and excited at the same time. He had been working so hard. What would happen if this letter too did not bring good news?

He was in such a hurry to know, he went ahead and

read the letter to himself, though his father and Sam Lock stood close by.

"Dear Chin Jin Mun,

"We are so happy that you wrote us. It was a terrible tragedy for us to awake and find Lew Wai Hing stolen. All these days we did not know where she was. We have mourned for her all this time.

"You have given us new hope. We do not have money to send you. We are poor farmers. But we do have a cousin in San Francisco. Lew Wai Hing will be surprised to know he is there. He left after she was stolen away.

"He has an herb store and is doing well. He sends money home to his parents and brothers and sisters. Here is his name and address. We are sending a letter to him also, to explain.

"Please tell Lew Wai Hing we are well. Tell her that we miss her and are so grateful she is still alive. We thank you for all you have done for her."

"Father!" Jin Mun burst out. "Come with me! We have to visit the herb doctor!"

His father looked at him, confused. "Why? Is someone sick?"

"No. Not at all," said Jin Mun. "You will see."

Red Means
Good Luck

Lew Hay Gum's herb store was just a few blocks away, but Jin Mun had never been inside it before. The air was strong with the smell of dried herbs.

A man was standing behind the counter when they rushed inside. Probably many people rush through these doors, thought Jin Mun. They are eager to buy medicines to cure their aches and pains and troubles.

After Father introduced himself, he said, "We received a letter from your cousin, Lew Hay Dai." Jin Mun placed the letter on the counter.

Instantly, Lew Hay Gum's round, plumpish face brightened.

"I have just received a letter, too," he said. "Such good news! You have found Lew Wai Hing!" The herb doctor bowed slightly toward Jin Mun and his father. "You have been very kind to our family."

"My son could not stand to see your cousin locked up. He likes the freedom of this new land. He thinks everyone should enjoy it."

Lew Hay Gum nodded and smiled.

"As soon as possible, I would like to go to this Wong Lo You and buy my cousin's freedom. Can you arrange this?"

"Certainly," said Father.

"How much is he asking for her?" asked the herb doctor.

"He is asking for $800," said Father.

Jin Mun was surprised. His father had never told him the price.

"I want you to understand I am not a wealthy man," said Lew Hay Gum. "I, too, must send money home. But I can pay her master now if, after Lew Wai Hing is free, she would agree to help me in my store for one, maybe two years."

Jin Mun nodded. "You will be pleased," he said. "She is a hard worker. She will be a big help to you."

"Good," said Lew Hay Gum.

After saying their polite good-byes, Jin Mun and his father left the herb store.

"Excuse me, Father," Jin Mun said, "but I must do something."

His father did not ask what.

With only one thing on his mind, Jin Mun ran down the street. He was happy. His plan had worked. And now he would tell Wai Hing the good news.

He passed the shops filled with hanging ducks and dried fish, vases and scrolls and scenes of villages. Soon Wai Hing would be able to see these things too. A red banner caught his eye. The Chinese characters for good luck were written on it in large gold strokes.

Jin Mun smiled. This year of the snake has brought us good luck, he thought. I'll buy this for Lew Wai Hing and it will be a sign of her new start in a new land. He ran even faster. Up and down the familiar hilly streets. Today they looked beautiful to him. As beautiful as any mountains.

ABOUT THIS BOOK

Red Means Good Fortune takes place in San Francisco during 1868–1869. Chinese customs and holidays were celebrated there in much the same way they were celebrated in China at that time.

The Chinese lunar New Year, which occurs between January 21 and February 9 on the Western calendar, traditionally began in the evening with a family feast. Other customs included making offerings to family ancestors, setting off firecrackers, visiting family members and friends, and giving "lucky money" to children.

The festival lasted until the fifteenth day of the first lunar month. On this last day was the Lantern Festival, when whole communities were decorated with beautiful paper lanterns. Processions were held, more firecrackers were exploded, and dragon and lion dances were performed.

I became interested in the Chinese immigrant experience in the Northwest when I lived in Washington state. I heard exciting stories about Chinese crews helping to build the railroads, and horrifying stories about anti-Chinese riots in the 1870s.

When I began doing research for this book, I learned even more. I never knew Chinese girls were sold as servants in this country; the practice continued into the 1920s. Nor did I realize the extent of the terrible poverty and starvation in China that forced some people to sell girls into slavery.

This illegal importing and sale of slave girls was encouraged by stringent immigration laws in the United States, called the Chinese Exclusion Acts. These laws prohibited many Chinese laborers and their families from entering the United States between 1883 and 1943. The laws also prohibited Chinese men already in the United States from legally bringing in their wives and families.

In my reading, I also came across accounts of young Chinese men who, working with a missionary woman named Donaldina Cameron, helped rescue Chinese slave girls. One such man later courted and married a slave girl he had helped to free. Out of all this research, my story grew—a story about the Chinese slave trade, the building of the transcontinental railroad, and a brave Chinese-American boy named Chin Jin Mun.

—B.D.G.